"Let's Grab A Margarita After We Cry"

VINA FLO-Glo

Table of Contents

Introduction 1
Chapter 1: Vina Really Did that 4
Chapter 2: We Just Here 6
Chapter 3: Highschool 11
Chapter 4: Marriage Life/Here come the kids 14
Chapter 5: Status is everything! 22
Chapter 6: Decisions to relocate South 24
Chapter 7: "Housewife to Hopeless" 28
Chapter 8: Beach life-Happy LIFE 33
Chapter 9: Blindsided 36
Chapter 10: Bullied Madness 40
Chapter 11: I Cant Make this Up 43
Chapter 12: Signs Don't Lie 47
Chapter 13: "Everybody Needs A NIKKI Brown" 59
QUOTES By VINA FLO-Glow 65

Introduction

This is such a phenomenal story that I've been wanting to finally get perfected and finished for all the Hardships, Joys, and Fat lips with Triumph that Life can blow your way. I've been told, "No way did that happen." Ummm, yes, it did! What do I mean? I want you to travel back in time and remember the Earth is still really the Lord and the fullness thereof. I want you to see from the lens of imperfection. I want you to think about where you could have been during this time and that time.

And you know what else? Think about what you went through in your own life experiences that may have prompted you to be exactly where you are from your seat. This Title comes from many aspects of life-altering experiences that make you think about heavy situations that were my story and my story alone. Why be so vague? I had a lot to protect in -the -midst of the writing. When you been a woman of my particular age (Wendy Williams's favorite saying), you have to be mindful you are capable of changing your mind. And so many times, I wanted to just walk away from all this shit. Quitting is so damn easy.

I say that in the most humorous way. Have you ever thought about suicide? I ask because so many say, forget it I'm out. As a matter of fact, I was on call once with a young lady who niece is dealing with depression and suicidal thoughts. We have all been there. Satan has a way of making you tripped up on life as if you are the only one facing the hard shit. Well, I'm here to tell you, "You have gifts the inside of you that somebody needs to be given." Be that gift I say.

You will see how in a moment "Life' was a bit much for me. And you will see how it's not a Giving up day, thought, whisper, or prayer away. But it is about Showing the dirty little devil you built for this.

So whatever else he is tossing, let him. You're Gods child and your God is Greater. Believe that! Believe it with your chest out, as Kevin Hart says.

    I thought I went through some storms. I'm still reminded of how God spared me from the hands of the enemy. Why do I say it that way? Have you ever been in a vulnerable toxic situation and thought, "How in the hell did this shit all of a sudden enter my life? Why? What am I thinking? What was I thinking? Well, I made it out. I made it out, and I promised God if he spared my life, I would not ever think twice about that scene being in my life again. I walked away unharmed but miserable of the thought. And that's why I sit here and type and reflect on the goodness and kindness of God. If he was good to me, what makes you think he can't be good to you?

    My heart gets so full as I remind myself on a daily just how God has allowed me another chance. Have I deserved it? I shake my head because I will be the first to admit "HARDHEADEDNESS."

    As you read and see from my view all the adulting I've had to do throughout my journey now, you most likely knew someone like me. And it may be yourself. The reason I say it may be yourself is due to the simple reasons of life, "we are human." I think that's another reason why I wanted the book to be in a relatable mode and standard with the title. Don't get me wrong; the title can give some people, as religious beliefs give, a side-eye. But I say bring it. All in all, I'm a Christian, too, and nowhere near perfect. I reminded someone of the 1st lady caliber and was asked the title because their church or husband is a publisher.

    Crickets were the sound at the title. We are so judgemental and will disguise it in the most obvious ways. Clearly, I never asked her to ask him, "The Pastor, to publish it." But she felt the need to make sure to share well you may want to consider elsewhere with publishing. Me, "I never asked you for input on my title and publishing." So, I said what I said. Title stays. Heck, if you think this title is off the charts of the prayer list, wait till you see others to follow. I mean, isn't art creativity? Then what is the big deal if someone calls something "margarita.'" All people have to do is not buy it or look into it and watch a flood of others turn the pages because something was mentioned to help the reader look deeper than the title.

So, journey with me as each chapter unfolds greater and deeper. If you want to know me, sit back.

Grab some popcorn, and tell Margie to stop by for a drink and get a box of Kleenex. I am saying this ahead of time. You will need it.

Chapter 1
Vina Really Did that

Wow, the graduation of the class of 1993 was truly one to always remember. I recall reading a speech and stepping off the stage, and I may have gone in the wrong direction when I stepped off the stage. Either way, I recall the Principal giving me a kiss on the cheek and saying my speech was perfect. Yes, in high school, we were troublemakers at the end. Why? Because they wanted to ruin our last segments of being a senior. So, I recall the Valedictorian was to be on her best behavior; no senior skip day, we could or else be reprimanded. I know, right? Senior year end-of-year blues factory. We made the best of it, though.

Fun times with classmates from gossip, who is dating who, prom dates, and college to-be. Just so much was this time and era. One of the many highlights I was prepping for at this time was being a contestant in the Miss Indiana Teen USA pageant. Yes! Me. I was mostly glad for the opportunity because it looked good, sounded good, and was good for my self-image and self-esteem.

Let me just say I was a well-rounded chick. I didn't have too many enemies; if I did, it was because they chose it, not me. So in, doing something of this caliber was like a breathtaking moment in my crazy 18-year-old life. The support and sponsors made all this possible. Even this was a big deal. If and when the pageant took place in Indianapolis, it meant you go on to the one that appeared on live television. I mean, who would run in the other direction? I ran to it vs from it. Silly I was at times. But again, this was that moment of winning or losing. It is parallel to life now. You win some, you lose some.

Okay, I admit I may have had a big head just a little bit. Not that I need it to be bigger. But I was eighteen. And at eighteen, either a few things take place. Party like a rock star all Summer, prep for college and goodbyes with last travels, save up summer job cash, and allow that to be the ticket to fresh starts ahead. Well, let's say I had a little bit of all 3. I know, right? It's true; I really did. Hey, I was "18" once, and it is now my speech to my kids. It worked for my parents telling me, so I used it on my kids. At least, I think they heard me.

When I told my family I was writing a book, they all responded, "Hurry up." They just don't know; I actually had been coming up with a notes strategy for a long time and placing it in my cell in the notes section. Also, my family just doesn't know, but I have so much to get off my chest to be real and authentic. They have seen me in real, raw character. Never to disappoint but to make laughter. I have such a humorous side.

I wish more people would laugh as often as I do. I will find a way to see the silliest in stuff on a daily. I've often used the statement. You would rather see me silly and cracking up at the dumbest shit or curled up in the corner and not know my own name. So pardon me with my laughter and unstoppable human-girl side of life. I told you I have been through some shit, and I mean it. So listen up. There are some funnies I got to share with you, as well as how in the hell I like the moments you are sure to read about me. I believe the best way to get to know someone is to ask them yourself. Can you relate with me as I make this statement? It's important to have an idea of whom you are dealing with, and I'm known to be a "clinically certified nut." I stole that statement from a dear friend's sister from back in the day.

Chapter 2
We Just Here

My family knows if I'm around and you see me, I place hugs on you and kisses. My mom would always tell me I had a way with people and relationships. I wonder if she meant that Vina was pre-married or Vina post-married. I think we need to ask her.

I grew up with three brothers, and I was the only girl between my mom and dad. I do have an older sister, who is dad's daughter. She lives where I was born. I was born in Beloit, Wisconsin, on January 23, 1975. I come from the coldest state, and I always felt like that as a kid. We had snow up to the door as I was coming up. Even when we moved to Fort Wayne, Indiana, in August 1986. Man, you think we were cold in Beloit. I stayed cold, it seems like. Adjusting to Indiana was a lot to get used to. I recall the church back in Emmanuel Baptist church having the annual Church picnic, and we would do our last goodbyes and send-offs from there. I recall the matching shorts outfit I had on, all the watermelon and BBQ, and the friends we all grew up with.

Saying goodbye as an 11-year-old kid is hard to do. Who will my new friends be in Fort Wayne? I thought time and time again. Where will we go to school in Fort Wayne? Will I see the other families and those kids I was familiar with from school? There are so many questions to ask and research when we are Hoosiers. Oh, I missed my grandmother on Mom's side. Nothing like those Sunday dinners. Daddy's grandmother was sharp in the kitchen as well. Just so many food possibilities. Ok, let me stop there to say, Yes, I'm a "foodie," and all of us like food. I mean, we all love food.

There were so many facets to adjust to while in For Wayne and no longer with the crew from my hometown. I know I used to enjoy the swimming pool at the apartments we had chosen to live in. I also recall being so built up in shape that I had a certain swimsuit, which was a 2pc. I recall the colors were navy, yellow, and white floral. It reminded me of vintage clothing from the 50's or 60's. My late granny Madear found it for me at a thrift store. Those happy moments shopping at the thrift store were everything to me. I wonder why I loved thrift shopping as a child or pre-teen.

Even now, as I reflect, the times have changed, and the big thing to do now with my 17-year-old is go thrift store shopping. Funny, to say the least, but it's true. So anyways, as summers were already hot in Indiana, being able to sim was a relief for us Davidson kids. We had parents that were particular about our care while they worked. If latchkey kids existed, we all were just that for the other. The boys always wanted to play outside, whether football or basketball. My oldest brother could hang out with his rascal buddies he bonded with. They were playing video games in somebody's apartment. Those twins and I were trying to finish cleaning and get to the pool. I mean, let's face it, they were about to go to kindergarten as we all started living "the Hoosier" state of mind.

Even as Dad adjusted to the General Motors truck and Assembly Plant over in About Township, he would still get off and see us at the pool. He walked up with his light blue shirt and jeans on. I think Dad still had a Jerry Curl in that head of hair. Yes, a jerry curl. Just thinking of the plastic caps on his head full of activators and oiliness is a whole mess. I'm laughing. If you had a jerry curl, you were labeled as "had it going on." We were so darn silly. What does that have to do with my book? The beginnings of life are in the newness of being in Fort Wayne. The school would start soon, and all I could think about was who I would get the pleasure of calling a friend.

I remember when we did attend a church and had a mix-up with Pastors. But that was cool be I did gain a friendship acknowledgment as we sat at the church we thought was the guy who had been to Beloit before and held a revival at the New Zion Missionary Baptist Church. Long story short, wrong Pastor and church. Oooh, but when we found him, it was that preaching man from Mississippi, and he was Pastor at Progressive. This dude could preach so tough and help you spiritually. I never knew he would be raising me and my brothers up over time to learn some more common courtesy ways and behavior. Here's the truth about a lot of this church family gathering, etc. We only knew of church and being a part of the things and events the church had to offer. Well, this Pastor and his family of 5 children were pretty much in the ages of myself and my siblings but maybe a few years off with his daughters. It didn't matter. We still connected to them, and they to us as well. My dad wasn't a big church attendee back then, but I know he believed in Jesus Christ. This family didn't treat us any different. They welcomed us and picked us up for Saturday Red Circle class on Saturday mornings. If there was a choir rehearsal, we would be attending that as well.

So, really, they became that loving family extended to us, and we needed them in more ways than one. So again, we were new to the city, new school, and new church. Just a new identity is a big thing in a new area. I thought I would share that because I still say it's a lot of who I am today reflected back to my youth days, which was upheld and inspired by what I was surrounded by. I held a major secret secret, though, and never realized it was that huge of a deal. I blacked/blocked out a hidden trauma that would also shape my world in major ways.

Growing up in Wisconsin, I realized I was the victim of molestation, continuing as repeated rape from a family member by an uncle. The harshness of being innocent and someone violating you as a child sickens me to the core. So, who knew after years of living and growing into adolescent years and adulthood, women had a lot to do with me first being a child? If you know of anyone in your family who is being raped and taken advantage of, called names, and or bullied by an uncle, cousin, or neighbor. Auntie, etc, please be brave and get that help you need. The silence of a child's voice is a destroying battle to ever reach bravery. Don't be so quick to say to a child negatively, "You tell everything," or stop telling on each other when you have siblings. Those verbal, demeaning, lashed-out sayings will ultimately trap a child in thoughts that no one cares; no one will help me if I ever say anything.

Because of the fear of not being believed. Parents, if your child has something for you to know, listen with both ears open. Another one I can't stand to hear. "she so fast" Ummmm, maybe bc she has been touched by a damn pedophile in the family whose and relative. Pay attention to the kids, and do not be so quick to dismiss and think the child is lying. Who else do they have if you are not on their side? I needed to get that out now before I jump further into the book "Let's Grab A Margarita After We Cry!"

So again, it is a new school year, new friends, and new adjustments totally. I never felt alone and scared all rolled into one. Why, I wonder? Maybe because the halls were bigger, and I was in middle school for 6th grade.

The school was taking off to start. Not as bad as I thought. We would have skating parties with the middle school, too. Talks of fun. I recall those precious days from our childhood in Wisconsin, crossing the state line to Rockford, Illinois, to attend the ING. Yes, the ING. My auntie Ann taught my oldest brother and me how to skate. I WISH GOD I STILL COULD SKATE. Seriously, hitting them curves and skating like no one's business.I recall even in Beloit in the summers, a dude would come to the lagoon and let you rent skates for the day.

Why in the heck would we skate from the lagoon to home? It was normal. I bet at least 2 miles was the distance. I tried to tell my kids how we used to go to the lagoon and have t-shirts made from the printing press shop. And please, do I ever recall Dryan's ice cream shop? We would get the ice cream, and they would also pop fresh popcorn. We would place popcorn all around that ice cream cone and eat it happily.

Memories are hard to forget. Even over in South Beloit, Illinois, there was a hot dog place, and Oh My Gosh, the relish made for the best taste. It was a privilege if we made a trip there and ate those hot dogs. The only thing I would say that came close to those hotdogs through the years was when Orange Julius was in business. That Polish sausage and relish and bacon bits w/mustard was heavenly.

Chapter 3
Highschool

It seems like the family visits were longer as time passed by, and we adjusted well over the years to Indiana. Dad bought us another house. Ikr right. From the villa Capri apartments in Fox Point Trial to the family home off of Standish Dr. Still is a part of the Paul Harding High School. We were known as Harding Hawks. Navigating that huge school to me was scary, huge. I celebrate knowing I had two good years with my oldest brother, so that's what's up. He was the football and basketball teammate holding starting positions. He and several excellent players graced the halls of Harding Hawks.

The rivalry was always the street talks of Southside, Snyder, Elmhurst, Northrop and Northside, Bishop Dwenger, and Bishop Luers, to name a few schools. But you know what? They have cheer blocks and pep rallies held at Harding, and being the fan of the oldest brother, I wouldn't change those dynamite moves "like Mike" on the court or football field. He ran, he scored, and he dunked. Those were memories I got to really see up close of my brother's basketball and football years.

I became class president in our Sophomore year of high school. That was fun and memorable, too. I was always told early on I exhibited leadership skills and qualities. So, I figured I would do this and do it with all my might. I didn't win my Junior year because the rivalry was very strong. All in all, it still was fun, and I still made an impact on the student council board that year. In my senior year, I was told I might as well run for Student Congress President, and I did. I know we held so many events along the way.

There was even a time donation I had asked people to assist because my aunt had newborn twins, and they experienced a house fire. The outpouring of love was impeccable. She was so grateful. I was not only pleased but knowing the helping hand of donations that helped and supported this was remarkable. I will never forget the teacher who kept Student Congress facilitated at Harding, known to us as Mr. King. He was a decent teacher and a kind human being. He didn't say much, but we all had respect for him.

Dating was fun during this time. I had several choices and fun with that part of my journey. I know, right? The joys of dating in high school and being selective. I think even now, I may have a selection from time to time, but I choose to keep it professional and not at the front of my mind any longer. I had to become this way due to nature. After you grow and mature over the years, you become immune to the games and unnecessary funny dating involved. Yes, as in everything is no longer funny when you are used like a pawn, abused, and not respected. Actually, my heart goes out to the generation now because they are getting all the drama. We didn't really deal with it in the manner that takes place today.

Oddly/Weirdly, the world has changed. But let's be real, I had my little sweet fun. Or should I say they had sweet fun with me and my craziness? High school was supposed to set the pace for college. Well, I always felt because I struggled to learn like others. It was mostly geared toward students who were destined to achieve high honors and such. I recall so many, many, many other students being so much smarter than me and probably still are. But over it all and through it all, I gave what I could. Even as I struggled in college in 1994, I had a hard time at Ipfw. It actually wasn't until the 2007 era that I could speak up for myself and realize I really had a learning disability.

Now, looking back, I realize so many curve balls with my learning and advancement levels never achieved, and all stem from how I learned. Even in middle school, math could not be tackled after a certain degree. It has to be a better way to make it come together. However, no one has been successful enough with me as a student to get the core grasping of fundamental concepts. It may be embarrassing to some to admit, but this is what is so freeing about me being transparent. I'm not concerned about being judged. Here's my take on all matters. Are you happy you have an opinion about me? Then carry on.

While in high school, I made matters just as bad. I can do anything else except the math stuff. I'm not sure why it's so complicated for me to make it work. It's my ADHD, I'm telling you. I know I learn differently, and it is going to be alright. You may be reading this and saying, "I can relate." I told you this book is about being relatable and making it all make sense on my end.

Chapter 4
Marriage Life/Here come the kids

I had the opportunity to move to Savannah, Georgia, where the world was truly different from my normal daily life. I had the ideals set in my mind one way, and then it didn't go as planned as well. But I think the experience had a lot of life moments to be attached.

Making the shift to come back to Fort Wayne was major. I wasn't expecting it all to come so fast, but we decided, meaning my ex and I did decide to just go ahead and get engaged and tie the knot. That's the American way, right? Don't get me wrong; a lot took place at the time. I was in Fort Wayne working through a temp agency and kept a job as often as I could and would. Another dramatic drama I don't even want to think about is the house/block shootings. Every time I think about God's hand being on my life and my family's life, we are all so blessed. I am blessed beyond words I could ever come up with.

All I know is that time and a wedding and new beginnings were a major turn of events. People often say what they regret. There are so many layers to that regret we can ponder in our own lives. But I believe I grew a trust in God then. And by the day to day, Trusting God with my life and family life has run deep. You know why I say that? I speak on it because the world can prepare you for the turmoil to come. The world can't prepare you for tears; the world doesn't care about the scars you get. The world is just the world.

We live in the last and evil days, and that's exactly what it is. We never know a day in and out what is expected. All we can do is trust The Higher power. My Gosh that higher power has had me in places where I had no choice but to trust him. U wouldn't believe me if I kept rambling on.

Just believe me, the Wedding and Union was beautiful. We did it! We were Mr and Mrs. Life, Life, Life. Arguments and oops, we prefer. I know, right? I said well damn! It's funny how, as I reflect on it all, I pay close attention to all the stories that carelessly and lovingly surround all we endured. Me pregnant. I remember personality changes and reading books on pregnancy and that changing body. Wow! I may have cussed a lot of folks out.

Yep, I said it. I remember my grandmother, who is no longer with us, said to me, as I was telling her I was pregnant, she said, and I really quote, "You just laid down." I thought I would roll. As a matter of fact, she dropped the darn mic. Our late granny Madear was a hilarious one. She was a jokester and comedian, and I mean, her funny bones were everything to me. It was one thing to recall being under her heavy arms as a kid. But it was something extra special to know she was just that kind of grandma everyone needed to have. A cook to her heart. She definitely smiled down on me during this time of my life, as I know she has always loved my children so dearly.

Back to new weddings and marriages, the Happy bouquet toss, and a baby on wedding night bliss. I'm just saying all this gives so many memories, Not all bad. I remember working specific jobs during the pregnancy, and just going to Doctor's appointments was huge. I recall how I was changing and learning my new body. We definitely were low on funds. Why does spam come to mind? Nothing like a fried spam sandwich when on a budget. But we ate.

Before you knew it, we were trying to see the sex of the baby. I was rooting, girl. Ex was rooting for my son. And, of course, being as young as we were and naïve still, I recall placing a layaway at Kmart and all gurl stuff. I found out again, another ultrasound, they said nope, a boy. Well, the exchange of girl clothes for boy clothes. We had to make decisions. I had nice stuff, though. Before you knew it, with winter leaving and spring being the better temperature, we looked up, and it was close to delivery. I know, right? Even as I reflect on it all, I sit and just think to myself, I am almost 50 years old. I've pretty much lived half of my life. My babies are all so big now. Only one left to graduate.

Hearing my blood pressure was high on a Friday was no fun. Memorial Day weekend on 5/98. Would you know I was sent home on blood pressure med that caused a headache and had to call the obstetrician on Saturday morning because I had no sleep? Told it would be baby weekend. In opposition to having him on 6/2/98. My life and Pitocin. Babe, I wasn't ready at all. I could hear that heartbeat and be checked, and it was only dilated to 2 centimeters. Maybe it was about all that happened. Miserable preparations to have a medicine cause contractions so you can dilate. I'm sorry, but science on that part is a piece of work. My little boy was not coming through the birth canal with the Pitocin.

I was miserable. So by that Monday, I told the Doctor, "Ummm, let me holla at ya for a minute?" I said, "It's agreed c-section." Let me get back on track; it was not the most pleasant feeling to feel the water break, either. That, I think, was like a long crochet hook to my visual on that Sunday morning. So not pleasant at all. Here's the bundle of joy story: he was born, and we were told he was 6'2 and 19 inches. I'm thinking very long. Dr told us we were not diluting due to the umbilical cord d being wrapped around his neck like a scarf. Wow! Scary, and I mean overjoyed to see my son. Handsome little fella he was.

Nursing was a trip. But I was told by others, if I could recall the benefits of it, "Please keep at it and let those 2 weeks pass, and he will be perfect for it." He was a sleepy daytime kid. At night, we would go round. I don't know why babies get scared at night, it appears, because, all nite, he would awake. Me- Dead to the beat of dripping breast. Man, you talking bout some day hour-long naps and singing to my boy. He was named after his dad. However, in my belly, he was always my "lil Stuffy." He's been our Stuffy since, believe it or not.. My dad calls him "Tuffy." Let Papa name the kid, we all would say. He did.

You know, as I think of the baby and all the new changes in life after c-section birth. I never knew the dilemma of weight and stretched muscles. I have told my kids often I needed J-Lo money. Pay someone to have the baby. Keep my tight shape. Yes, there was a time when my shape was a "Coca-Cola" bottle. It was the "brick house." My type was a flat stomach with no waistline till I looked back at pictures like Lil girl girl." They weren't ready, and indeed I wasn't. Even after all, the c-section births a stretched stomach muscle. No, ma'am, could you ever get back to that pre-kids? I know, and I wish it wasn't that hard. Over the years, I did my best to maintain at least looking decent.

Back to the born and no-sleep life of my little stuffy cries and healing the pee-wee and navel button. I was on top of organizing and making sure he was swaddled and clean from head to toe. I mean, if you were to look in the diaper bag, you would probably detach tags bc something was always extra packed in that bag. I had so much. I recall the church giving a baby shower at the Pastor's home. Those were the days when it was so safe to be a guest in the Pastor's home. Now, you can't pay me to sit at the man of God's home. Nope, that chick any longer. I believe everyone needs space to retreat as they wish without being up under a microscope all the time. Don't get me wrong, even my childhood Pastor, from being brought up in Fort Wayne, had the most loving home and atmosphere. Heck, we were all his little shadows. Real story. Never a dull moment in the home of my Spiritual dad, who reared me and so many others my age.

I was the favorite one, though. Yes, remind him I said it. Seriously, motherhood was fun, and even being a wife had its highlights. I think over time, as things begin to stabilize with myself and my ex, kid one and kid 2, and Lord comes Hollin' Molly Toots. She was a temperamental chick. I would be the type of mom who let a child cry it out. If I had two others with homework, dishes, and housework before Mr came home, then I had to do as I needed. If I slept all day- good luck. Taking care of a much-needed, well-built home with love and noise and all the creeks of steps and rain hitting the window pane if it rains is meant to be productive.

Yes, I had the opportunity to be a home wife for the 1st seven years of my son's life. He needed me a lil' extra. What I mean by that is simple. He had many health scares as a baby, beginning at eight months, which led to asthma and bronchitis. If you never had a nebulizer machine in the home, pat yourself on the back. Indiana was known for asthma, allergies, etc. I don't think there was a winter at all or a season where bronchitis wasn't a health issue with my son. His age now of "25" amazes me because he doesn't get sick.

And if he does, it's a shock because it's like, well, what are the symptoms? He's so tall, has the same skin and tone as me, and is handsome as ever. My 1st born, that head turned. I have to make sure vultures aren't trying to pry next to him. I have a hard time letting them all grow up. But being a high-functioning autistic Adult with Aspergers, I have to break stuff down to logic and illustrate examples for him so we are on the same page.

I will say this: he's skilled at basketball and has completed his Associate's and Bachelor's degrees in college. I'm most proud and forever thankful God allowed him to be able to be at the Campus of the University of Central Florida for the past two years. He earned them scholarships for dorm-apartment living and a Dean's List as well. Smart young man, for sure. I believe lots of prayers kept this young man. I could not do it alone. I taught him prayers as a child. And I also taught him to know God for yourself. Actually, it was a blessing to be able to teach all the kids this. I tell them often, as long as you know you can press play where God hears your prayers. Believe me, he does. All you need is access. Access is a believing, willing, and trusting heart. Knowing the Father and Son Holy Ghost are real and rules our lives even when this wicked world has a hidden agenda. Take God's word for what it's worth to s scriptures right in the path of destruction, and watch God deliver.

Giving birth to my 1st daughter in 1/2002 was a big deal. Let's keep the laughs after the C-section delivery. I swear they switched my baby. Why do I say this? b The ob-gyn knocked me out or signaled to the anesthesiologist to do so bc the tug was overrated. I remember seeing her on my cheek. And how pretty and hairy she was as well. I looked up in recovery and my room later, and all these little spots were on her. I said they switched the baby. Would you know lil gurl was rocking her "Ralph Lauren' pale pink pj's, but all her clothing had never been washed?

So, the pediatric Dr. whom I love dearly and respect tremendously, said those are stork bites. She was allergic to the dye in the clothing. Who knew? I thought to myself, "MizzyPead2does," already acting bougie and just said Hi to the world. I declare my parenting stories at times get me by the "throat." The real meaning is the throat. Because no way you would believe me if I told you. So this other little hollering kid is now a part of the "Welcome to the family bunch." She was a sweet baby. She ate very well, and I nursed her too. I was able to nurse her for at least 10 months. She was taken off due to the cortisone injection shots I needed to have done quickly, soon, and fast after a long, hot summer and follow-up appointments as well. I placed the shot injections off long enough. We even had the opportunity to go to Disney World when she was 7-8 months while our son was a toddler and discovered the Buzz Light year sagas.

You know, I think back to that hot as-ever summer and think as far as Indiana, how that heat then was scorching to me. Do you know what I did to help us get to Disney? I knew I could cook well. So, since I had the time, I began making grilled chicken salads and taco salads in my kitchen and told a friend to say to a friend. I recall saying a business means a business. I looked up, and weekly, my little diet 7-up cake slices and million dollar pies was an awesome dessert with the salads. Can you believe $7-$8 is all I charged? I mean, beauty shops would place order after order, and the women's shelters had busy workers patronizing them as well. I was doing very well.

What about the toddlers and infant troopers? So, as long as my son had a Buzz Light-year in hand, a transformer in the other hand, and a case with Hot Wheels cars, he was the perfect babysitter across my front living room with the door locked as I would go back and forth to help him potty and take orders from the kitchen phone. I know, right? It was the perfect setup. I remember my mom said she went home with my dad to 2 salads, and he said where did they come from? She sat back, eating hers, and uttered, "Vina's kitchen.'

Let me be honest. I recall my mom had a few days off, so she insisted on coming over and helping me start the setup to stay organized. Major help that was. Why the seven-up cake as Diet 7-up? Well, my ex was diabetic, so I made sure I did this just as I needed to accommodate him wholeheartedly as well. Let's face it: I was the at-home mom, and sometimes, the dude would work both shifts because of the duties. They made the seats for GM, so when GM was off, they were off as well. So, summer getaway breaks were of the essence, especially because a shutdown prompts a vacation. I didn't care if it was Kings Island in Cincinnati, Ohio. We spent two days there letting the kids' splash around. Then, we drove over to New Port, Kentucky, and went to the aquarium.

We lost Chaya about 90 seconds at the New Port area walking mall outdoor area. We let our son do the bungee jumping and were thrilled to see that. Her hand was on a stroller when the last baby was born, and she let go. See what happens when you have a big responsibility for more than one kid. Thankfully, she was crying in an outburst, and people gathered. We turned around and retraced the steps, and everyone from the store managers had her consoling her. Now, I have never been a parent who wanted the strap on the kid with a backpack/handle. But I damn sure get the underneath message. I was a scared ass woman.

My ex never showed panic, but that day, he did. I swore to always keep my kids close at all times, no matter what, and that's why I preach to them now about Keeping and staying close at all costs. "We are all we got." A significant family statement. Now, everyone has grown and is moving in their direction of life. I jumped around a little bit, but I promise to include the last birth down the line. I've got so much to get off my chest.

So, to encourage every woman who had to choose to be at home as I did, I applaud you. As willing workers of the home front, I know it's never easy, but we ultimately make the obvious best we can and hold it down in so many ways. It's a job that doesn't get the recognition it deserves. I advocate for moms who have to take a little time to raise their kids the right way/ that's always a big commitment in this world. Husbands have a role, which is leadership and providers of the home—breadwinners, we used to hear. I know the idea is not always welcoming, but I will say to adjust as such to benefit the entire family constantly. I truly believe we did make the right decision at the time we had with focusing on the family.

Chapter 5
Status is everything!

Who comes up with this shit. Let me wrap my head around the status. Where in the world did this come from? Who started this dirty little trend of backache? Tell a lie on the tongue, jeepers, creepers, a load of shit. That was a mouthful, and I had to get my thoughts out. I come from a blue-collar family setting. My dad worked over 30 plus years at General Motors. Somehow, we were thought to be rich or not the needy, yet all of us were greedy. I bet we knew the struggle was real. I had the opportunity to work at General Motors back in 1995. I was lucky, so I thought.

I swear my fingers would hurt after being on the motor line. Daddy came over there to see me as I was starting up, and his shift ended. I couldn't even complain; it would let him down. You know General Motors HR played favorites. It was hard as ever to get that application from the gate. So again, working 2nd shift and maintaining self-respect and dignity was a lot. I had to represent well. AND DID!

I look back at the summer as if I can get a do-over, but knowing damn well it will never happen. General Motors, car rides, drop-offs, and blasting music to make it to the 469 highway and be on time. I mean, that line waited for no one. But it was a nice learning experience. All that time, I have still been trying to find myself. What would I do after summer's end? Where did the time go by the time July 1st week and 2nd week showed up? VACATION, Man, I needed it. Time waits for no one at all.

I was so young. Wet behind the ears, smelling my shit. I know I shouldn't swear. Well, write your book and say what you wish. Do as you like. Im Vina, Im telling my story and the shit was fucked up. Thinking back to the pluses of the drive, gas may be $.79 a gallon.

Shewed, you could drive to Chicago, get a hotel, eat, and party on the drive-thru of the skyway, watch fast cars, listen to party music, and make it last forever. Those were the days. My goal is not to bore you but maybe make a lot of what was racing in my head even then a relevant and relatable conversation.

Chapter 6
Decisions to relocate South

I won't peddle too far backward after a major economic setback and building a home we built ground up after honing in on the finances and all. It was actually very memorable, and lots of prayers. I think this is another way for God to show us exactly who he was and what he did. We were attending one of the churches in Fort Wayne, Indiana, which really represented a bible-based word worship center.

Here's the joys of it at that time. My last kids snuck in out of nowhere, and I swear I was not supposed to conceive anymore. I thought it was a wrap. We were so done. Nope, the escape artist had other ideas. I knew I was trapped. I mean, the aches I had with that kid in the womb were unreal. I can't recall if I was able to take Darvocet religiously or what. I know we would go grab my grandmother, the late Granny Madear, and keep her fresh and fed in our basement with blankets so we could make sure she was warm. My kids loved her so much. I think back to the days we went over to her apartment or the house she was in at the time, and she popped their popcorn. They loved her spirit and character toward them. I have to admit, she was an example of the epitome of a real grandmother.

How do I explain a lady who may not have had lots to others, but in our world, she had everything? I wouldn't have ever known her to be a lady who struggled financially. She used what she had to see it fulfill the kingdom and her home. So, being able to assist her in her later stages of life was more like an honor than a chore. I mean, for a grandmother who lacked in so many ways, from the world view of not having enough, she still relied on God and Jesus Christ to meet her and everything. It's sad how we did move later on down the line in time, and we will discuss further the hard decision my mom had to keep making for her care. I know she would consult with my aunts, but ultimately, she had to make the decisions.

My kids would make her laugh so much. I'm telling you the joy of laughter was this woman's ideal of living. We were blessed at that precious quality time, as I know it. She wanted us around, and that meant so much. So my kids understood her needs and care wasn't as simple as ours, but never did they ever turn her down to want to hold her hand and be right under her. She became their world as well. I used to love to hear her call my son "Chucky." She would call Chaya "Shy,' and I think she would refer to Chania as "Doris."

Yes, the last child had my grandmother's name as her middle name. My ex was always willing to assist her, which was sweet. I think his being close to his paternal and maternal grandparents was a way he stayed connected to the elderly. It actually didn't matter if it was family or not. It's just how he was raised. I used to have a hard time knowing someone needed a curtain hung in the rehome. He was always going and never saying no at all. I believe there should be limits. I will always believe there should be limits to that. I have my own thoughts on those matters only because of what hand I was dealt.

We did separate for 22 months back in 2007-2009. Ironically, we got back together, sharing the laughs of our last child. She was rather funny, And I mean extra, dramatic, just always into something. It's funny as I write because my son would always chase her out of his room, messing with something. She was that kinda kid. She also was an asthmatic kid. I recall my middle child having tonsils and adenoids removal. We were told by the ear, nose, and throat Doc to make sure my middle kid didn't run and get exerted. Well, maybe she did a little bit. When I say, blood was everywhere.

Let's just say My granny Madear would say, "Getting tonsils taken out just about makes you bleed to death." Ummmmm!! Lots of facts. I was covered in blood in the ER. They had to sear it, and I mean quickly. She was a mess. And in the in-between, the last kid was having an asthma attack. I thought, Lord Jesus, please come down and be of comfort and strength because I felt weak just having my kids checked out in the ER and then back home to rest the nite. So yes, the ex and I figured out a heart-to-heart conversation at my table in my apartment and said ok, we will attempt.

But I also said face-to-face that I'm not dealing cards on anybody's table if there is another separation. I'm keeping up with my end of the agreement and will file for a divorce. We eased me back to the home we built and kept it moving as usual. He decided to get back into school and enter the medical field. At this time, I was a student working for a well-known hospital in the city on the north side of my hometown.

Funny knowing how I can talk myself into anything that will be a blessing to my family. I had the opportunity to meet with our security operations manager, and my nursing manager needed me to show him some information about our stock room supplies. Well, lil ole me had the opportunity to first acknowledge him as a former chief of police or lieutenant or something. She said that he had leaped at the chance when he got that call for the operations manager.

I said to him in these words as he thanked me for the stock and such, "I have fewer credentials here as a unit assistant worker and have been trained." My husband has a whole lot of computer programming under his belt and has had the hardest time getting a job here. Why did this man tell me to have him go back under the site and apply for a particular position and give him a call once it's done? Why did my ex at the time do what I instructed him to do? We looked up, and his start date was a matter of days away. See, I told you I play fair. I will do whatever I need to do to adjust for my family if it means it will be a blessing in the long run.

But now my smart-ass side of life is like, my ex probably thinks I did something to earn that place of employment for him. I evaluate so much now and realize if I was accused, watch where the finger-pointing came from. Guilty others. Well, it was given in a matter of 48 hours, which was a totally closed deal, and an interview with a drug test. The reason I say that so boldly is because I have been in positions where I had to prove I knew what I experienced and witnessed and made it happen. I don't want everybody, and clearly, everybody doesn't want me. Some conversations are so innocent, and I mean it truly. It was a part-time spot, but it was a foot in the door at least.

Why did I downplay my education or skills and say his was more qualifying? I said that because it was a fact. Not to take away credit being due to the other person. Now I see that in a different light after all I have been through. There was a time in my marriage when I was told to keep my day job. Well, hell, my day job was keeping up with our kids. So, to some, that meant that was the job I needed to keep. Well, to me, that wasn't funny. I strategically kept an attitude about it, and I'm capable of being so much more towards it. And I had to apologize even to my inner self for my stinking thinking.

See, when you land a hospital job, the ability to train is often on the table. I'm not referring to professional positions. So, I had to learn to adjust my mind and renew it. After years of feeling as if that was a rejection, I wish someone would downplay my skills. What are my skills? You reading my book, right? So don't let anyone place you in a box as if you are incapable of succeeding in other areas. You won't go far. Yes, the bad stuff is easier to believe, and it projects out of the mouths of others toward you.

Chapter 7
"Housewife to Hopeless"

This chapter will dig a deep tunnel to see just how drastic the challenges became transparent in my life. Moving to Dothan was hot weather. Don't get me wrong, I knew it would be, but I mean, it was aggressively hot. The look back on all the heat in the air, adjusting to the new apartment, and the new bugs were one thing. But it was little more than that early on that had a lot to do with my mind and the mind of the marriage.

Notice how I lay this out. The reason I say pay close attention is because it is a thriller. The thriller is so intense that I even wonder why I'm exposing my truth. So, as the kids ended the school year back in Indiana, it was our time to be south permanently. You know, now, as I think back, counting lots of debris that already wreaked havoc on our life and marriage at a time or two, it makes me think about the thriller already in the creeks and crevices of the marriage. You see, my ex had the opportunity to be in another area without the kids and me for about 90 days. Would you believe that very place suffered a major inclimate weather of tornadoes that ripped thru the area?

Being I was the wife at home and still organizing, decluttering, and giving away items, you'd think I had time to pay attention to the path of destruction that played in our marriage as signs. I didn't. When you are that type of woman, such as myself, you tend to brush stuff off for sanity purposes. I know I have to explain. Let's just say my mindset has to be completely thwarted with evidence to show me I should be doing or watching for something else. I have stuck in my ways syndrome badly. I never want to believe the obvious. At least, that's the former self. Now, I don't put anything past anything to make sure I'm seeing the light.

So how did all this marriage dissolve is the obvious question. I recall once this all took place with the move and I took my gurls to Memphis to be at my aunts for several weeks to get them away and bond with her. Having that opportunity to do so was one of the sweetest bonds an aunt could grant her great nieces. My gurls were so excited to go to Memphis and spend time with family. My son and I held on closer to the pool because the heat was so hot. I mean dry heat in Alabama. We even thought he was stung by a bee or wasp in the water, only for me to see absolutely nothing on his back but the sun beaming down. I knew it was time to get sunblock SPF40 quickly. We all had tan lines quickly.

So again, the summer of 2011 would be a new start with us here in lower Alabama. I realized something was different between me and my now ex. I couldn't place my finger on it, but then it became clear. I said this niggah ain't touched me, had me touch him, etc. Something off. So, as I said, when I suspect a rat, I'm looking and lurking for clues. I got the thug to open up. And did I…. If you don't mind what I'm about to say, good. If you mind, good. Did he just say what? Come again. Actually, partner, you haven't been coming here, so where have you been? Here, the icing on the cake of all affairs. I'm turned off by you and your c-sections of our kid's birth, and when he works to assist the at Rehab with baths, it is a big turn-off. So, wait a minute. I swear all I see is Bernie Mack's big white eyes and his phrase, "way-minute." I said what the fuck did you just tell me.

I guess at that point, I was supposed to appear ashamed of my excess weight gain and join in the shame game. I said hold up, hold up. Who is this trick bitch you are dealing with? Because, at this point, I'm smelling all types of foul odors. One thing about us as women that I've learned and paid close proximity to is we usually can pinpoint the lie, threaten the partner, and close the case on a verdict. I went crazy. I'm looking for cell phone bills and everything. Because in my defense, you are not telling me the whole truth. I said the verdict in, Yo ass guilty. And it's clear.

Why was I told they were gonna get an apartment together and I could continue to stay where I was in the three-bedroom with the kids? Why, my daughter said I snapped so hard that she saw me with a belt in my hand, and he hopscotch the hell out of my apartment since, now, I'm the renter of the apartment as a matter of fact... The jokes are grimy. As a matter of fact, this joke is so grimy that you think I'm a fool to laugh.

Now I'm ready to hurt somebody. Hurt HUMILIATED, BROKEN, BATTERED, Emotional distress, call 911. Hell, I am 911. I was the call to action on the scene and was ready to hurt anything of the opposite species. Who moves their entire family to some shit show, catastrophic, pathetic hot, ass city in a circle ass city? And we have been here eight weeks. This means no sooner than I drove back north to see you get started without us while we let them finish the last month of school in Indiana, you had a happy-hoe-down good ole boy=good time. Yep. The title looks like you are capable of saying agreed.

Why isolate me from my family like this? This is some pathetic low-life, back-alley hogwash in my book. Oh, I'm the author/writer, so yes, as I said in my book. My feelings were to fuck him up! How, I don't know.. I called the heffa. And did, of course, wouldn't come out of hiding. That's the thing I hate about affairs; you are bold enough to handle them and aren't bold enough to HANDLE them. I was so furious I felt like my astigmatism, which was a crooked eye/leans, had straightened itself the hell up so I could see straight, think straight, and retaliate on the least of it. My emotions were all over the map of shock. It's a wonder I didn't wreck my car. I was driving my "96" Lexus then. What did he have to say? What in the fuck do they say? Looking crazy. Or I guess I showed out crazy for real.

Do you know the day I found out that it was Dad's birthday? All my family was surrounding him and having a celebration in Indiana, and I was on the cell phone snotty-nose, and I mean pouring tears.

Everything I thought about hate hit a nerve, and I became. Everything I ever thought about assholes hit the last nerve. And, of course, anything that ever had the balls to say was unattracted to me, and I had 3-c section births and honored you in the marriage, hit the last nerve over the last nerve. The pits of hell I thought could have him. Take him. Get him out of my damn face. I'm all embarrassed and here with no damn next of kin.

But I'm a ryda bitch. So I begged him to make love to me, and I meant it. I wanted to be her since she had him, "My husband wrapped around her VJJ walls," then make love to me as you do and did her.

I do not recommend that no other one go this deep. This part made me made me throw the hell up. I threw up so bad I was sick all nite. I remember calling and speaking to my mom. All I knew was that she had heard me, and I felt ill just describing the scene. It was very dark and low. But I thrived from hurt and lots of layers of that hurt. In that moment of disgust, I realized that whatever made me sick to my stomach pit was a spirit. This is why I do not have intimacy now. I live celibate. I don't want all of them. It is dangerous to be at this point in life. I want to be able to recognize me and not have to identify with anyone else. You see, I know me. I don't know her. Nor did I want to.

Oh, I know I'm speaking as if she is still around. Is she? I can say I'm still around. I don't have a clue. I'm shedding light on my entire ambushed situation at relocation time. This shit is fucked up. Yes, I cussed; please get over your feelings about it. I said as I said it, and then as I relived and pried those layers off, I cleaned up one day. But it isn't on any other terms. When I learned that Jesus still loves me during the dirt and grime, and he still does now, as I illustrate, you see strength.

I remember speaking to someone before about how you love hard and forgive easily. Me, I did that. Let me say, "pick and choose what suits you." I cannot confirm nor deny it won't be comfortable and painful together. This means that when you numb it on the inside, you are liable to be posted up as anything. It's called fight or flight in psychology. I had even met a dear friend who pointed to me. Since you are in this situation, let me show you where you can go and get assistance to feed the kids since he is playing house over on another street. I was happy to do that, at least.

No woman should have to feel some way if her spouse is no longer attached to the marriage. How will the kids eat, live, and bathe? Now looking back at the time of war and how hard I had to shift my mind to either like him still, love him, forgive the crap, look for coping ways to make it all make sense, and pray like no one else had a problem to God but me and my situation. You could not pay me to think that's how my life would end. As I showed so much transparency and vulnerability, I wanted others to learn one thing: Amid the struggle of what blow I was facing, I still looked to the hills from which my health came.

See, God loves us all. It's the sin of this crap he hated. We eventually were somewhat in patch-up mode and trying to heal through the harshness of my new area in which he chose us to leave and live in Florida a year later. We had to shift again. When I tell you this setup, remind yourself. I said to take a break. Where I'm leading, this will blow your whole mind about our lives.

Chapter 8
Beach life-Happy LIFE

Notice the title. Well, there's a lot of stuff to still mention. I hope you were able to take a break and sit silent with the rest of this.

He decided there was a window of opportunity in another county, but now at the edge of Northwest Florida. A city we never heard of. But more money and the house we were told we could rent was absolutely immaculate. I mean, this house had every upgrade we didn't have when we built it in Indiana back in 2004. Listen in and listen up. You do know that I was still a stay-at-home mom with my bratty kids, and that was the choice.

We were in a rural area. The prison sat not even 3-4 miles from our beautiful rented home. Hers the truth about this home in cost survival. We only paid $700 for rent in a beautiful brand, newly built ranch-style home with the highest vaulted ceiling I've ever seen. The kid's rooms all had their own walk-in closets with plenty of space. The guest bathroom sink had Jack and Jill's sink as well as ours. So let me help you visually with the structure of the home; it's built-in stucco, which down here is the best-kept hurricane-weathered material, etc. He had his own closet, and I had my own.

We had a stand-alone shower, and I had a darn jetted jacuzzi tub. I faithfully took baths in it. I mean from the lightning to the foyer front door glass brutal storm door with pane glass stained, two car garage, and sizable back yard. We even purchase an above-the-ground pool. And needed it. It is hot in Florida. Mind you, we were an hour from the beach to Panama City Beach. Eventually, I got a job in Destin, Florida, to help with odds and ends, groceries, and such. It was an hour's drive. That morning, speaking with Granny Madear over the calls was so enjoyable. I would leave at 6 am and arrive right at 7 am. I worked from Wednesday-Saturdays 7-5, and

Saturdays were only till 1. It had advantages because I could drive my kids with me, and then we could hit the beach in Destin for the rest of the day.

This was glorious for me and the kids. We really did become beach bums over in Destin. So many of my clients at the time had got me acclimated to San Destin as well. My son was able to meet a heavy-weight boxer whose ear was bit off back in the day. We still have his picture in my cell. I was able to meet contestants from "The Voice" all because of the position I held. We even had the opportunity to hear "The Voice" contestants sing in the park connected to a winery. That was totally up my alley. So, as you see, we were still taking strides to make it all make sense and work. The kids and I even discovered this big church on the highway. Someone told me of it as well. We went several times and had my ex with us. We later learned they were launching a prominent spot in Panama City Beach. Well, by this time, it all was so worth it.

You see, I'm a woman, and being a woman, I don't look for fights and arguments just to be nitpicking. Now, if you come for me, make sure I send it to you. It is very important to know that when I come up with what I know and will do, I must make sure you are ready. Yes, I said it. I promise I will add more to this before I take it back. So that's how we got introduced to Beach Life, which is the happy life I thought. Keep in mind the closest grocery store from the rural era home was every bit 30-45, depending on which direction. I fell in love with Publix. And I have been buying from them now all these 13 years. Also, at the job I took in Destin, I sat on the sidewalk to Publix.

So I could grab and carry the ad home as well. Believe it or not, Publix was the 1st job my son had as a young teen, and he bagged groceries right there as I worked on Saturdays he also did. And as I said, Beach was our exploration. I do rave about Destin, but I recall that it was a happy time. Packed outlets to shop many sights. We would always encourage family when they would visit and drive over to Destin; it's worth the shopping we always enjoyed. The restaurants, too. Be ready for the next part.

Chapter 9
Blindsided

Around April 2014, we decided to move towards Panama City Beach, Florida. Well, just like that, I recall adjusting to his new job offer. But I also had just had major surgery. See, this surgery was brewing since Fort Wayne when I couldn't walk because I found out I had a fibroid the size of a golf ball. You know what? I don't regret having the surgery in March 2014. What I hate is I suffered in silence for so long with the condition. To actually see there was light at the end of the tunnel was refreshing. But on that new heal-up mode of life from a physical ailment that was desperately needed, I had to adjust my mind to the latest and nastiest news. What I am about to help you follow with a timeline will not only make you side-eye me, but you already know I don't care at all.

What I care about is being free from the ridiculous laughter I had to endure and feeling a torturous way in my path of "How in the heck can I escape this?" Remind yourself as you begin to see a lot of vulnerability and transparency that I'm just one woman. This happened too. There sits across the globe, and many other women have endured this and maybe worse. I say this because people are quick to judge and get it twisted, as well as misconstrue that someone wreaks havoc on themselves. In most cases, what has happened in our (my) life and those of others is an act of blindsided narcissistic behavior.

First of all, I do not agree with narcissistic, gas lighting, and manipulation behavior. I think it takes up too much time and effort with thoughts of negative persuasion to pull it off, and others will ultimately be hurt by it.

Mother's Day that year was a mess. There was the discovery of a conversation on the cell phone between my ex and the other woman. The person who made the discovery was heartbroken to display the information with that being said. When the discovery was made vs. when I learned of it, it was most likely a three-week gap. See why it's important for you as a parent to never say to a child, "Stop telling everything," "You are talking too much," etc. Kids have to know there is an adult they can trust. In this case, it just made the entire matter worse. I can't make this up. You mean, not long ago, on one of many riding home nights, I heard a song, came home, and it was taught to my kids, and praise and worship began to be sung in our home.

You mean to tell me the prayers of the righteous availeth much scripture just went out the whole window? Talks of throwing the whole going to church thing away again and again just made me question what I choose to believe vs what I believe. You mean to tell me every fiber of wanting to make my marriage work after the 1st affair has just been slapped in my face.

Would you believe a nine-month affair was the highlight of the monster? Who in the hell moves their family to back alley woods, still in rural areas, and has time to make booty calls? Who does this? Well, in my own sanity and own defense, I lived this horrible mess, even a nightmare with axes, belts, knives, jackhammers, saws, etc.; I thought to myself, what the Fuck? Just what the flipping Fuck? Mad as ever. And then made out to be the one crazy to my family. This sickens me even more. I guess I am crazy. Because if I had any of the above-mentioned devices, it would have hurt someone. How much was my heart supposed to take, endure, suffer, cry, mourn, destroy, and, of course, be bitter from?

I'm so far from perfect, but this just placed me in shock. Who and why would someone think so callous to do? The roots of Satan's destructive path are just pure evil. Heartbroken was not enough to even come up with. But even then, I downplayed my feelings so much because my kids meant me keeping my head in the game. I knew I wouldn't be enough to satisfy this man or his new needs all of a sudden, and I refused to compete with it.

We ended up on the beach and 2000 feet steps from the sand, and there was so much I couldn't think to say. All I could go off of at the time was that I had the opportunity to see my kids enjoy sand castles and make mud pies with sand. The beach itself was just tranquil. So when you think about judging me, think really hard. This same setup could end up at your doorstep one hot summer sandy day, and you will do your best with what you have to use what you got to survive.

I was even in counseling with a Pastor who I have a lot of respect for. She made the comment to me, "But you chose to stay." That statement was one of the most hated comments ever made to me. Choosing to stay in my mind was a plaque. How in the hell could I get rid of it? Who will assist me if I needed? But my kids' thoughts are just as important when it comes to keeping them in close proximity to their dad. So you see, choosing to stay and having the card dealt this harshly towards me, and I hated it, but it only made me sit tighter as long as I could. Forgiving him this time around was the roughest decision ever to face. This is asinine at this point. There is no rebuttal to this, but the game plan and escape should be done when the timing is right.

Time went on, and the church was a great distraction. But deep within, losing my God conscience mind, I swear. Now, don't get me wrong, I purposely sat behind the Pastor's family every Sunday. As a matter of fact, he was just a cool guy. Just thinking back to all that and that era, I'm glad his wife allowed him to be in our life as he was. That church grew so quickly. I've never witnessed something so beautiful. I mean, every Sunday was the best. The kids were enjoying the children's church. I was enjoying greeting and all. I think we were amicable about what happened.

I forgot to mention the finding of the text was so bad at the time of 2nd known affair that even the child was accused of lying. I had just bout lost all my shits at that point. So, as you can see, I had so much to do, Phathom. I had so much to take in. I had layers of understanding that I had no way of knowing how to understand it all. Being a mom who protects her kids and sanity in matters was tough. I masked it as best as possible. To me, I did as best as I could.

Let me let you in on a secret: when a person goes through something so traumatic, we question the realness of even our own bodies, makeup, and characters. I know you can relate. That's why the title is so catchy to me, "Who in the heck wouldn't want to Grab a margarita after this here cry?" If I could make this up, I would. I can't. It did happen. I lived it. I'm a survivor of abandonment and gaslighting that utterly tried to destroy my health, livelihood, and thinking.

I used to think if I had been educated, this couldn't have happened. But here's the truth. There is no amount of education money could buy that could keep you from facing such destructive behavior prompted by someone wanting you to lose your holy mind.

Suicide, I thought, would never leave my mind. In my life, I have felt what the point is. I'm not on drugs. I might as well be. I'm not an alcoholic. I should start. But I still kept going to church no matter what. It ached; God knows I was ready to hurt something. And anytime I could be there with doors open, I would be there. The shift in youth leaders started changing, and it messed with my kids' interactions with those whom they gained trust with, as a child's heart is so pure.

That was hurtful for me to see. Other than that, I have nothing bad to say about the church home we helped launch here in Panama City Beach. I couldn't thank Pastor and his wife enough during that time either. They were from the Louisiana area, and he would always refer to Boodrow jokes and Katia. Did I mention there wasn't a time I never sat at his church, and it was as if a fly was on the wall in my life on a weekly basis? I mean, how relatable could his sermons be for me to hear and receive something from it?

Chapter 10
Bullied Madness

As I get you prepared for my job, life, and style on the beach, be mindful that you have to come inside something that I don't wish on my enemy ever. And I'm not one who has enemies that I have up close and personal knowledge of. When I say learning the leasing industry was a form of sales, I possess what it took to be successful. I'm not as quick a learner as most, but if you give me the time I need and a detail-oriented focus for my brain, I can successfully accomplish and close the deal. Also, keep in mind how this was an avenue of decent income. Income with salary amounts and commission on top of that and apartment with a discount.

So, my last eight years, of 2024, Christmas time till June 2022, I was at an apartment complex as the head leasing person over time. I had responsibilities that meant we ate, shopped, and traveled as well. Disney World on a budget is possible for a resident here in Florida. Disney cruise was also made possible. So, I'm most proud of those much-needed vacations. Any time a parent can take their child out of the country and return safely is definitely a sweet memory.

What I had to endure to be able to handle at least a vacation is a whole nother message. First of all, if you see me with a stare on my face, you look confused because I am. If you see me in no-comment mode, I don't need to say anything. If you are in my face and your direct hit is to aim below the belt while you are on a rampage to embarrass me, please go right ahead. If you ever asked me directly if I had anything to say after you vehemently tried to shred me to pieces with your war vocal antics.

And my stare is still a look of BITCH, you crazy for real. That's because BITCH YOU ARE CRAZY for real. Sorry, not sorry for the last statement; it was your honor. In other words, harshness in the office was a bit critical. I begged the Human Resources team to come to restrain this crooked tail lady. They pushed under the rug.

And finally, on the last straw, after so much of the riff-raff was just dumb anymore, they sent a team to investigate. I think I was written up by this time, and yes, being me- I refused to sign it. Signing it means you agree with it. I am far from stupid. Look here, once all was held in question and all was cornered with being witnesses, absolutely no one stood with me. You know why they fear their own jobs being in jeopardy. Here's my true case and point to the matter.

No one in the rabbit-ass mind should have had to endure the bull crap I was dealing with. This office was overrated and disturbed not only by the manager at the time. Her husband would get out of pocket on my Saturdays working, and he would still come for me. I told you earlier in the book, If I send for you- come. If I don't send for you, do not come at me. At this time, he was a resident with a chip on his shoulder. Looking back, obviously, I was always the kitchen table talk because, believe me, he would treat me like shit in my face, around my back to the side, or wherever. She was cruel, and he was just flat-out a dumbass.

Needless to say, all that stress later and so forth, eventually, she was moved off the property and sent to Orlando for a property. As far as me, I still stuck it in as hard as I could. I've never seen a witch brew the way she used to brew, whether I was in the room or not. I could come to work with well-groomed clothing on and ironed to crisp; hair and make-up were perfect.

Residents would make mention of a positive comment about me; she would shoot it down like it was a plaque. She still couldn't stand me. I look back now, and wow, did I have a glow around my life that she wanted to disrupt that badly? She was a tyrant. People would come in there with gifts for me. She had a problem with that. Nothing I did was good enough. So all this, and I'm struggling to stay married to a man who still showed and demonstrated I wasn't good enough for him. My life sucked big time. When my family came to town, I placed a happy face as best as I could because I didn't see any other way. Hurting inside was miserable. I can't even make this up.

I used to have mothers of newly graduated college adults show up in my office, and I just needed the mothering nature of a woman such as myself to peek in on their adult kids from time to time. I would because it was respectful and safe. Please don't say I was the favorite on the property too loud. That boss would lose her shits. I recall one family brought me a lighted décor for the home that she would make from time to time. I was so receptive. I loved it so much; my mom told me about it on a call one day, how it "lit up my life," and the words I heard from the resident's mom about me "lighting up their life." I melted. She made me another one, believe it or not. I was able to share it with Mom, and they still gave me another one. It's the prettiest thing ever.

This main event here, I promise you, is what started a series of uneventful matters that took place with me in the office and away. I promise I can't make this up.

Chapter 11
I Cant Make this Up

I had to recall so much harsh stuff to get to the brighter days. Back in Summer 2016, it was harder. I recall wanting to truly focus on weight loss. That was yet another catastrophe. From work to the gym was my life. One of the residents offered to help train. Well, his background was navy, so choosing that poison as a figure of speech was "put in the work." My mom's brother was ill in Memphis at the time, so road trips were of the essence.

I have to admit I love a car ride and sit back to enjoy them often. It's a calm for me. Most peeps rather fly, and that's all good when it's a long haul. But for 8-15 hours, I'm game for a car and highway window down and hair in the wind. I want you to know I was a busy chick, and having spaghetti legs with lunges and squats was a trip. But I applaud the trainer because he would devote himself to me and his girlfriend four days a week consistently. Well, immediately, I was accused of an affair with him. That was crazy. His son was little and being watched by my daughter, so it was a barter/trade for you to help me. I can help you and let my daughter assist. Y'all, when I saw the shit hit the fan, and then I was gifted a car in the back alley of the fitness center as I was sweating and running and flipping tires.

Back then, I would post on Facebook to enlighten and motivate others. He had jokes. Here's the funny story to that. Have you ever seen Micheal Meyers or Jason from Friday the 13th? Ok, so the mask would appear from every angle, trying to catch me up. The joke began to be so funny one day. I was at work and realized the ex was never at work. He had allegedly gone to somebody and was given stress days off. Me, say what? The spookiness was getting rather serious. Now, don't get me wrong, I was at a serious place in my life where I was doing more for myself. Something I never had the mindset to completely do before or at least a long time. The tripped-out part of it all was when I knew all my girlfriends near and far had been called and told by him. He was sorry for all he did to hurt me.

Ok, that's a lifetime movie; I'm bout to die; I knew it. Well, not yet. But believe me, all of them tight-knit girlfriends began to fear for my life because it was rather disturbing and suspicious. It was so suspicious I couldn't tell you half of it.

An old saying says, "RUNNING CIRCLES AROUND YOU." This was my life. Ratchet, I was at the time selfish with regard to my own needs, I guess. And blocking out all the spookiness. I even recall the trainer stopping at my job and clearly making a threatening remark to let me know he was concealed and carrying. My mouth dropped. The picture I'm trying to help you see is this. No matter how much you begin to invest in yourself a little bit, it's gonna be an issue. You could be going back to school to finish your degree.

But if there is any inclination of jealousy amongst the married couple, trust me when I say someone in that marriage has an issue with the advancement of the life about to take place for the spouse who is trying to elevate. Besides, any time a spouse goes to any great length to get your own flesh and blood to turn against you, it's a catastrophe. Counseling was off the table because I didn't have a problem. But if you are me and go into the shower and step out of the shower and darn near break your neck stepping over a grown human being because now you are trapped in the bathroom and can't leave because the door is completely blocked. I thought to myself, this cannot be real.

Who has the time and energy for such drama? Story after story. Situation after situation. A woman can only put up with so much. And at any rate, a woman of my status who was kindly working well at the apartments every day and leasing apartments. I had made decent cash coming in to keep afloat. I was saving where I could and still went back and forth to Dothan to get my hair done only because my beautician was not here on the beach. I still very much patronized her.

Keep in mind I had been getting my hair done with only one income. Now there are two incomes, and being red=flagged as if guilty pleasure gone bad. I cannot make this up. Even if I asked my stylist to come here, she began to feel threatened. And that entire situation went way below the belt when she did come and was feeling some type of way. I had no idea my parents were being called in the middle of the night when I would do early drive-ups to Dothan. The mystery was revealed later. As I still digest all this and find the words to grasp from all the details, it definitely was a hard time for an eventful saga to take place.

When I was sick, I was supposed to continue to get sick and weak. Mind you, getting sick was icing on the cake for the next part of this. When it's hot here in Florida already, you are trying to remain professional at work, be a mom at home, and be somewhat of a wife because so much was itchy and sketchy all summer. I even said leave.

Mind you, a cell phone was tossed in the pond the summer before that. Yes, another cell phone that wasn't mine. But it all began to make even more sense that this marriage was about to dissolve. And at any moment, it could happen. I wasn't supposed to make friends at work or in the community, where I lived and served quite a bit with resident activity functions, etc. I asked him to please leave early on. I knew the satisfying factor could no longer be what would keep us together. You can't make anybody love you when they don't.

So here comes the torcher of the entire game of cat and mouse. Before I get to that, please know when I say Narcissistic behavior is something I never ever want to endure again. Please believe me. Gas lighting and reverse psychology are just as bad with man-ip-u-dippers, best known as manipulators… I can't understand why the control is so much a game of the mind. I'd rather you exit over to the right and just leave me alone. My patience and tolerance for dealing with gas lighting woes are not working for my energy vibes. The hardest part of the next chapters is knowing I survived what should have killed me, and, I mean, killed me. No way should I have survived this damaging psychological thriller. There is not a day I don't think about all of it again and again.

And there still isn't a day I don't say Thank you, Jesus! I mean that because my fear is that another woman wouldn't have been able to get through this as I did. My fear is that a child who had to see this so harsh being done to the parent somewhere in the world wasn't ready to go into a rage of terror and uncontrolled behavior all because of the home life being on maniac force within.

As I get ready for the next chapter to reveal some bad seeds implemented in my life, make sure you take a hard look around and make sure who you are married to is what you dreamed of and not what you need to wonder about down the line. One thing for certain and two things for sure: no way was my mind ready to be at the stage of life and prepare to come out from it. I was very blessed to come out with few bumps and bruises, but the greatest of it all is knowing I had some critical choices I had to make, and I was determined to live out what I needed to live out no matter if I did lack something in the long run.

Chapter 12
Signs Don't Lie

Go with me on a journey of the unthinkable. I told you when I love hard, I forgive easily. And because of that, people can take my purest and rarest form of love for granted. That's a huge lesson I had to recognize in reflection mode, looking in the mirror and crying one day. So, any woman or man who has a tendency to love with their whole heart, be prepared for the unthinkable outcome that could happen to you just as it did me.

I begin to have pain in my upper right area above the chest, close to my shoulder. Let me just say that I was diagnosed with diverticulosis a summer before from stress-related, and it showed up in such a painful way, so unbearable. I saw a gastroenterologist doctor, and even now, I see him once a year if I need him. So, this pain was some of the worst pain I have ever felt. If you pressed it, I was wiggling about to hurt someone because it was featured intense. Y'all, my boss pressed so hard one day it made me tear up. So here I am at work with this pain out of the blue and no knowledge of what it could be. I recall ER visit #1 and them really thinking gall bladder.

What in the heck does the gall bladder in the abdomen area have to do with the shoulder upright chest? Ok! The hospital did labs, which are your normal labs. I was even scheduled to pay all this money for a hida-scan. Ok, now I'm seeing a specialist on something that no one has found and pinpointed. I believe I was suppressed with pain meds and told to follow up with primary care. So, my primary care was a female physician assistant, and I loved her so much. She listened thoroughly, and yet she was helpful, and still no answers. I still worked out maybe a little here and there because the pain was a mess and very unbearable at times.

What was wrong with me? When a woman is in pain and we have endured deliveries with C-sections, etc., we know unbearable pain. I said earlier I did get to push my babies through the birth canal, but I nursed them little brats with all my milk count. Would you believe there is still no relief after the 2nd ER visit? The pain and 3-4 am wake-ups were something pretty harsh. Painful till I would be in tears looking for heating pads, etc. Cold compress as well. Getting ready for work was so tough. I walk to the office because my apartment is on the other side of the pool, and it's close to the office door. My boss and staff were amazingly kind during this time. My former boss was assistant property manager at the time. They couldn't figure out why the screechy sound was still forming in the area when I felt this pressure, and it was too much at times to fathom.

So, I had a 3rd ER visit. I begged them for the pain meds. You have to be careful when you are a pain med seeker because they think you are looking to get high; well, hell, I was at this painful point. They are looking at my history; I'm whispering in pain. My ex is sitting there with me, too.

Can you believe "blood clot" was the verdict? Just as I let you into my life, I want you to understand how bad it was for me to sit up on the ER bed and have the Dr. tell me in a loud voice, Mrs. Stevi, you are a ticking time bomb. I said what do you mean? He said, and I was startled to pieces in tears in pain. He said A blood clot is present, and you will be here a few days with Lasix so we can help you heal. Now, I'm told that most don't know this; clots don't necessarily disappear. Do you know what it means? They don't go away. But can be treated. He kept apologizing to me over and over again. He explained that he was being admitted and had nothing to worry about. They would take good care of me.

As I type this, I still see him in the scrubs attire and chart in his hand, delivering the message and saying they would order up meds to get me started through the IVs, IV's IVs, etc. When I say I was crying yet rejoicing, I could get better. My nurses were every bit of calm and nice. I'm one who pays attention to bedside manners, And they all had what it took to care for me and my illness. Believe me, as I say, I know what I'm talking about where bedside manners come into play because even now, one of my most endearing guys is also a physician assistant, and he possesses traits I feel every real man of a genuine, humble place should possess. That's a whole additional story. Stay tuned.

So, I'm the patient, and it took a lot of patience to heal and be in the hospital with a roommate. I know, right? It was a life-altering experience, and I recall she was older and a bit disturbed because my entire time there, she was over the top loud, from hearing the TV to talking to me and having phone conversations. She had a lot going on. So, how long do I get to stay in this facility and be cared for? At least 48 hours, I recall. Mind you, as I talk this through my mind and keyboard, I'm very clear on many details.

It seemed as though he was still doing some crazy thinking and behavior, and I recall my best friend in Dothan said to see if the nurses could ask him to leave me alone. He was stressing me. But I was still a little weak in forming my words about that. It was bizarre and scary as I unfolded to you the truth of the matter. This dude decides to go and buy a car off the showroom floor with my debit card with quite a few thousand dollars on it. When I say I was already confused, my healing needs the care and direction of my team, not thinking of a damn car. When a woman is fed up, there really is nothing you can do about it. I knew that my release day was August 6, 2016.

Well, that happens to be my dad's birthday, And with compassion, I recall letting Dad know I was going home. My dad uttered that it was the best birthday gift he could receive, knowing I was headed home. So not only was I trying to get discharged, but I was still trying to understand why the urgency of a new car, and he had just brought me a guilty gift car not even two months prior. So much assine behavior, I kept thinking. Recall my kids are home waiting on me to feel better; the dude had my purse and cards with him. So I did have to leave it at the hospital and risk it being stolen. I do remember being discharged and just so thankful they helped save my life at the hospital that I begged to go to the beach for just 2 hours.

Mind you, I was supposed to do anything heavy lifting and still ordered to bed rest. I begged the Doctor if I could go. He agreed that if I was safe and not swimming but enjoying my feet in the water, I wanted to relax if that makes sense. I felt in the hospital that I had quality care, but the beach was that thing that was relaxing for me. You get awakened at the hospital and poked so much I just wanted to be focused on the beauty of the water. Everyone knows my take on the water and the tranquility it possesses.

So I sat Thanking God with every breath, listening to my Bluetooth music, and watching the kids play with their families. I was so glad to be alive and had no idea what really happened. I knew he stressed me in the hospital because of control and such, but something about that ocean just made me feel alive and well. It's hard to turn away from the beach life, the happy life, even when moments are so unpleasant. Healing was a process in which I had to follow up with doctors' offices from blood doctors, who are oncology and hematology teams. I know, right? Who knew I'd be seeing what we classify as cancer patients' physicians? Well, I had to see the cardiologist as well. This thing was so close to my heart that I could see why they said ticking time bomb. Here's the truth of the matter as you follow along. I was not sick; I was until I realized how sick I was.

Guess what? My symptoms were still acting out. What? You read, right? I was still in the struggle to heal. Why was this little story so significant, you may wonder? When I say I was at the ER again. Please count that as 4th time. When I tell you I have a fever of 104, what is really going on? Now I'm tripping in my head. I can't be awakened in the middle nite of this hard pain, and it catches me surprised with the pain constantly.

The ER treated me> I explained how I had the fireplace, throw blanket, and ceiling fan on at the same time. I couldn't make this up if I tried. How bout I went back home and edged back to work? This pan of time was getting crazy. Recall they were supposed to have me pinpointed so I had the correct care to heal. I don't know that part at all. Time went on, and would you believe that at this time, in the middle of the night, I was madder than anything? I said, let's drive down the way to the other county and see if there was some way we could get answers. Please, people, please listen up. It's 4 am again.

I'm about to call off work. Because I was messed up, I think I was not scheduled to see follow-ups till a three-week window, which is close to the wedding anniversary, I recall. Ok, now this looks crazy suspicious. If he beats me to the doctor appointments and I'm like, maybe coming to drive me to them, don't you think? Then it got crazier because, by this time, I was so frustrated and cursing.

You are probably wondering why I didn't call out to God. I did and revealed a lot. See, we as women have this gut. Mine's real round. I say that to be funny because I had C-sections, and it left me with a bigger gut than I thought I would ever have. So listen in. Not only did I follow my gut, but I began to stare. If you beat me to the appointment and I, the patient, clearly way over in Panama City on the other side of town, I think that's fair to say, "I SMELL A RAT!" Did you forget already up top, I said I couldn't go to the other county for the ER.

I was told, let's wait. Wait, what are more symptoms? What's to wait for? I'm sick of this pain, and it's hard to bear. When I told you at the cardiologist appointment, I told him, please leave the waiting room; you are stressing me out. He sat. I said, please go. I got this. I will see what the doctor says. He sat again. Eventually, I thought he muscled up and left when my name was eventually called.

As God was my witness, I had to address as told by the nurse, and the doctor would see me shortly. As I'm describing this story, imagine my face as I type and think back to the cruelty this gave me. If I was waiting in the room from the doctor after the nurse did vitals and the nurse left, my name ain't Vina. The doctor comes in. And silent, I sat and then walked into the doctor and introduced himself to me. With that taking place and answering questions, there's a knock on the door. People, people, people, I could have jumped off the darn table. Knock at the door was him. He comes right in. I shook my head. I couldn't believe my eyes.

Remind you I'm smelling a rat. I recall my bestie telling me all the time how I set the scene. So here I am, basically dressed in front of the doctor, and my ex walked in the room as I sat at the table for my exam and questions. I said to him, even then, you are not supposed to be here. He stayed seated. We argued the entire time leaving as I heard what the doctor was advising of me, and I prepared to leave. I'm in disbelief now. So my hematology appointment, I never told him where it was or when.

Can you believe he's tossed my mom in this by this time? So, on the day I met the blood doctors, my mom called me as I was in the office filling out all the documents. She thoroughly questions me as if I am 10 years old versus 40-something. I said to her on the call in this ruff tone, "No way does he need to know where I am and for what? He's too suspicious of me. Something is way off. Has anybody not heard me say he trapped me from going to another county for the ER to look over me?

Why is the stall out? Was it because they could see what the initial problem was altogether, or what? Something is not adding up. I had all my girlfriends ready to come and go with me to appointments, not him. I begged the blood doctor staff to please not disclose my location to him. They respected my wishes. Why was I having this uncertain feeling? When I told you I called my physician assistant team, I begged you to call me back. I received the call at the close of business day.

She, whom I named Billie, was on a call with me. I had someone in the car with me going through a rough time, and I drove her to get an ice cream cone from Mcdonald's and explained this was something I did with my kids just to take a car ride. So the Physician assistant listened to me thoroughly. She encouraged me to sneak to the office the next day to have a urine test submitted, and they would check for all metals and anything abnormal.

Finally, somebody is listening to me. My job allowed me to do just that. The next day, I snuck down the road and to the county. I was trying to get to the ER area and was halted. She held me and said we will get through this. When I say I had to tell my mom because everything was so suspect, I couldn't keep up with what was next.

What were we looking for? Was my mom on board? Remind yourself he had brainwashed and manipulated them so badly to turn against me like I Was the rampage daughter out of control. He did a major number on them to manipulate them terribly. All I could do was wait and see what the results revealed. I called many days later, but there was nothing, and I kept watching my back. Pretending I didn't have an appetite and stuff just to avoid home-cooking meals because he had been fixing my meals for well over 3-4 weeks. I was exhausted and in pain. In need of relief. I needed someone to understand I was fighting a demon.

So I got a call from "Billie's office. She ordered me to leave work and get there immediately. With the urgency, my staff told me to leave now... I drove secretly, mind you. I wanted to do something to shed light on matters. I got there and was placed in the actual doctor's office in a nice chair as she sat behind her desk. And here is the news I need clarity on. She uttered to me she had been in a debate with the actual doctor of the office because clearly, the numbers don't lie, and she could see why the hospital missed the diagnosis she was bout to tell me and share with me.

When a patient is in the hospital, they order a urine test but not one that has extensive lab results with metals. Because I brought up what if I've been poisoned and had no idea? Brace yourself. I'm staring crazy in the face of her notes and her mentioning this is gonna be worse before better. I was declared as having arsenic in my body. Yes, it showed in my urine test that she ordered extensively. My mouth dropped.

She said clearly this was "rat poisoning." In an instant, I'm looking perplexed. And she insisted I would like to help you understand the findings. I knew no one would or could believe this here mess. I didn't believe it. She went on to tell me that the number was high enough to raise questions. I'm baffled by stares, and my mouth frozen open in disbelief. She then let me know of another patient who went through this just recently, and the wife was poisoning the husband. What we should have done was have a plate of food brought down and tested. Because we believe it was ingested. When I said there was no way, I knew how I got this mess in my body. We started looking up the symptoms and such. As disappointing as this story seems to sound, I loved it. Please understand following the gut does not lie.

She emphasized the importance of a nurse in nursing school following her gut and, in this example, following her own gut because she was right with this one. She even volunteered to call my mom and dad. This was the part that was hard to discuss. She made my parents understand that she trusted her guts on this one, and there was no way I had done this myself. I'm sitting there in tears. This lady was a doctor but instantly became a confidant to me. She said if you need me to hide you and the kids, you got me.

If I need anything, don't hesitate, and she even blessed me with a large amount of cash and told me it's important to be safe. Listen, money, hearing this, and being speechless is all a lot to understand what was happening. She said you need to go to the beach police now and show them my findings. I was scared shitless. I was losing my mind for real. I was in terrible shock. How do I play this off? My mom told her this was real. You do watch the news, and this is real. You also see the dateline and 60 minutes, 20/20, etc. She said your daughter didn't concoct this. She has been poisoned, and it's enough to cause the symptoms and such. I promise I heard a pin drop in that silence. She said to my mom I believe your daughter is smart and will do as she needs to do for safety matters. She said, and I back her 100% and encourage you all to do the same.

Please understand that I not only had to digest this news, but I also needed to get back to the CSI crime lab on my end of the beach to report the findings and make sure my kids were safe. When you deal with detectives, they interrogate the crap out of you because you are a suspect as well. Listen to this: not only did I report it and have computers confiscated, but they picked him for a lie detector test.

Well, I eventually learned lie detector tests don't even get used in court findings and evidentiary. So, how was this supposed to be true? Was it possible? And how can we pinpoint him? When I say the Board of Health picked up the findings, I was too thorough. I was called and didn't recognize the number at all. They had tons of questions.

These are questions I never thought of because why would I? I had no idea it was even possible to have this now hanging over me. Bizarre as it was and sounded, they also asked about my place of employment because if I'm drinking the water there, so is the rest of the staff. When the dude was questioned and picked up from his job, I had to deal with that, too, because we lived in the same apartment and shared the same bed. I didn't care if something was off or suspicious and wanted it to be handled.

The lie detector test mysteriously passed the test, and of course, they went through the entire computer laptop. A mess. He asked me, carrying the bible in his hand, "I can't believe you would think I could poison you?" My smart-ass mouth didn't rest; I said, "I'm looking at satan himself." And I knew I was looking right at Satan. I still admittedly keep my stance on that even today. So yes, allegedly, those were the findings, and I'm still not backing down. The board of health wanted to know if I had had wine or shellfish lately. None of that I had eaten or drank during the duration of this.

When he rushed into the bathroom as I bathed on our anniversary to give me a plate of food, I was so side-eyed in the view, thinking, "Boy, I ain't eating nothing. You are serving no more." This was still in the testing period of the urine test.

As I sit and think back to how God spared my life and kept me safe through and through, it is even a hard pill to swallow how I got here. He even uttered my co-workers had given me arsenic. I looked at him as if he was really stuck on stupid.

It makes matters worse; I was snapping at the neck so badly, saying things such as he got to get out of my house, and I'm serious. This is my apartment and has got to go. I was receiving a discount because I was an employee. I didn't care at that point if he didn't leave with nothing on but a wife beater and pair of pants. Why did I have to sit tight, maybe 10 more days till Labor Day weekend, and he would sign off my lease and be gone?

Listen up; I DIDN'T GIVE A RATS ASS, JUST GO. My parents took all they could to strategize and calm me. You have to remember, my parents were all I had and my kids. Why would you want to drive a wedge between us? I never called his mammie or pappi during all the excess calls he was doing, sneaking in the middle of night calls. I even recall a female cousin who came here and stayed in the guest suite apartment and told stories she uttered to me about her marriage and what the kid's dad did to her while she was pregnant.

Listen to me well, why are we making excuses for a serial cheater? I am not hearing this mess. Like whatever you uttered to me at those summer visits as she came over here from Alabama, never a relevant position for me to hear her. There was no respect there anymore. I recall asking why I drove a wedge between my parents and me. His reply is that he doesn't have anybody else. This thought was sickening, calculating, and guilt-driven. My world never was the same that day or night. It was best we were on different turfs and co-parenting the kids. Leave, please. Can you just hurry up and get out? I didn't care if the outdoors was the new residence; just hurry up and leave. My peace had been robbed.

You wouldn't believe this, but during the last ER visit, I was given Dilaudid. Yes, the med of a narcotic. Those narcotics they gave to cancer patients I recall knowing back from my years working at the hospital. I was in a lot of pain. So, if you know that now as I tell you the story, also take a deep breath and know all my symptoms disappeared. Dissipated, as they say… Now, that was a major relieving victory of the pain. I slept with a large butcher knife under my bed for a long time. I wasn't playing the game of being attacked. I had too many sleepless nights and feeling perplexed…

My Physician assistant had placed me on a med to help with anxiety. I know I ended up on Prozac at one time as well. When the move-out day came, and the police were here to escort the move, of course, I was at work. I had to work. I made it up in my mind I didn't care if the entire apartment stash of furnishings was gone. I wanted my peace, and that meant to keep out, keep going, and stay out. Yes, I could hear God say vengeance is mine; I will repay. But at that time, I couldn't find a scripture quickly enough. Hurt, dragged through the tumultuous betrayal more than once, was enough already.

I recall a time when the Pastor of the church we were attending tried to intervene, and the Pastor politely asked him to give me space and let me think. I had to call that Pastor back because nothing I had him to help intervene with was even looking optimistic for my peace. He just kept nagging. In my space, in my face, wanting to talk. I wanted silence and completely leave alone time.

Nope, I can't stand to be ignored. It made my life a living hell. I also recall a friend calling me, and I couldn't talk at all on the phone because he wouldn't let me be alone on a call. I sat in the bathroom of the girl's room, doors locked and bathroom door locked, running water and shower water with a towel on my head just to cover up the noise of a call. Does that look crazy? She told me that day, Well, you crazy? If that's what you have to do, just have a chat." I said well, maybe I am, but there is no escaping this. So, not only am I feeling tortured by my living. My friend in another state calling me stupid. Those words cut just as deep as someone telling me in a counseling session, "Well, you chose to stay."

Chapter 13
"Everybody Needs A NIKKI Brown"

This chapter will say so much. I've brought you into my life with clear, concise evidence of how the enemy attacked my mind one day. Not only did the enemy attack my mind. The enemy attached itself to my marriage and became bigger than the years built into the marriage. I won't wish the negative pressure I faced or endured on even a nemesis. And the last I checked, I don't have many enemies. But let's be clear that not only did my marriage suffer brutally, I had to be in a position with my kids to be able to hear them vocally.

Keep in mind that even their precious minds of them were "kid interrupted." My kids have come first for so long, and it matters to me that I can be upfront with them and leave an open-door policy for them at all times, no matter the cost. The rebuilding of our confidence in them was thwarted all because their minds were nowhere at the maturity level to understand all that took place.

As a mom, your goal is to nurture, cultivate, love, and sacrifice in ways you probably didn't receive as a child once. We have a responsibility to make sure they grow and succeed in life. We have to instruct them so they are not taken advantage of. We have to make a stand in our home so they understand that just because you have less of a rule at your dad's home doesn't mean that the rule I have here is out the door.

See, I don't play that. Nor did I see at all I could compromise and expect the ex to be on team Vina's parenting style. You can go to counseling, you can be in court, you can be on your own land, and you still don't get the respect you deserve. The statement that it takes a village is accurate and true. Kids are impressionable. Their minds are just age-appropriate as they may act. And quite naturally, some are progressing a lot slower. I would like to think my kid's minds were shifting through the adjustments as best as possible. I tried to be fair. I also tried to make sure I was lenient; it was only due to the tiredness, of course, I felt often. I didn't ask for my ex to stand with me on anything. I knew off hand asking if I was in need. In other words, I kept uproars at bay as much as possible.

If we went out of town, it might have been a switch-up of weekends or something handled simply. I just didn't have time for the extra noise and cursing out all the time. Recall I need to enter my peace zone as quickly as possible. Why do I mention peace as I do? Because you just don't understand the ramifications surrounding being uprooted from your normal and left like you were supposed to die along the route of life, especially after I suffered as I did. Nothing I went through, sat back and watched unfold, loose friendships along the journey, and could have been spared.

Damage was done. Words spoken. Lies told. Thieves stole, etc. You don't leave your upbringing and think Someday, I'm gonna share my story and be heard. No one wants to hear the baggage you carried. No one wants to think abandonment can happen in a marriage. No one wants to think about an at-home wife who should have a sister and instead be left gullible. Here's the truth to all this. My life is far from a fairy tale. Do I know I have peace of mind? Yes, I do. It took me purging so much stuff. Holding onto memories that need to be scattered at sea.

Purging from jewelry that meant not a shine could keep. Purging from documents that only kept a signature and last name meant no quality of a name suitable to be inked, penciled in, and written as if the line was safe to write on. Purging from items that you thought you couldn't live without. In time, you discovered that it was never meant to stare and never use. See, in my purging phase, I also had ways to get rid of weights that once weighed me down.

Purge-Purge-Purge. I learned to get rid of so much junk that couldn't even add up to "don't worry-be happy." I purged friendships that came back into my life and only meant manipulating me more. I had to set myself free from being used like a rag that was only used at the convenience of others. I'm not to be conveniently your safe space when you never created a safe space to be kept.

Over time, I realized that because of what I was willing to get rid of, God had a way of showing me that he could and would supply all my wants over again. I wasn't missing anything that kept a mediocre mindset. He had a way of elevating me and expanding me in a shift that I never saw coming. Just as I thought, I lost it all. God did show me I was only gaining my true self in him. You have to go through something sometimes so you can be wiser if it tries to destroy you again later in life. I had the opportunity to name this chapter after a dear friend of mine.

When I say it is possible you have NIKKI Brown in your life, you can. Her name may be Malaysia Copper. And at any rate, if you follow along, you will see the connection and may already have A NIKKI Brown in your own life. This lady not only took me to the office but I was being thrown under the bus by a former manager. She did her best to get me hired at the apartment complex where I had had the privilege of working all 1st eight years here on the beach. She is what you call a no-fuss type of chick. Loves her fashion, purse, and shoes. Yes, all top line. When I say this chick had the experience of being in the shoe industry and knows how to shoe shop comfortably, she does. And did and still do. She begins ordering my shoes out of the goodness of her heart to give me comfort. And because of that

I began to have high-end shoes on my feet, yet I could walk in them sweatless. So, I am calling this chapter after her with her permission only because I know she appreciates the honor and on mind, as I mentioned to her. She would go out of her way to accept payment as I could rather than pay her credit card back from my checking account or debit card, etc.

She still made sure Stevi's feet were comfy, cute, classy, and often. Did I mention one year, she reached out and gave my oldest daughter a bag of old, slightly worn shoes? All high-end. I told ya, it's nothing for her to high-step and look feet pretty. She also possesses that quality about her. Lunch dates and mani-periods are at her expense, often with my kids and me. So, pardon I mention her name. The purpose is to get you to understand she was the beginning of angels that poured into my life, and they kept appearing.

Why is the significance of her name mentioned? "She's an angel." From that moment forward, purging and ridding the items I no longer needed and dropping them to Goodwill were all part of my destiny. Eventually, people begin showing more grace and mercy with gift cards to various restaurants and activities. I'm not talking about just $25 gift cards. I'm talking about $200-$300 worth of gift cards. You tell me how this was not possible? It was very possible. My kids and I ate well on this beach.

One of the most significant gifts I had the privilege of being surrounded by was a lady who showed me so much jewelry. I purged stuff for others prior to seeing this angel come in one day, and she kept coming. Each time she came, I was sending boxes out of town, gifting the items away. Why, you ask? If I had more than enough, why be greedy? There was no real point in keeping it all to myself. I would call people and get their addresses, drop them off at UPS, and send them away.

This lady worked at the Navy base and still showered me so much more. She loves jewelry so much that she changed up often, and her path crossed mine, and into the office, she appeared again. So, trust me, I never ran out. I would love it if people could come into my office and say they just wanted to bless me. My eyes would tear up because I know God never ran out of anything. I even had the opportunity to allow a specific church women's group to have ur summer kitchen at the pool for a fellowship.

A 2-3 hour window it was. Guess who sowed jewelry into those ladies? You guessed right. I did. It didn't cost me a thing. I rented it under my name, and they were never charged a fee for the summer kitchen. I may have even made a dish. I just wanted to help. Over time, the guy who would come with gift cards was tying the knot. His wife and he still kept showering me with more and more gift cards. Sometimes, I would fill out an envelope and bless another person to go have lunch. See, angels were surrounding me.

My dining room table was brand new and gifted to me. I also received a brand new white bedroom suite. I had called on my navy guys and airforce guys and other neighbors, and they moved it into my apartment. I gave away the girl's twin over a full bunk bed, and my dining table, which I purchased back in 2007, is still in excellent condition. I gave it away. Not only did angels see bout me. But God had a way of showing me to pay it forward to bless someone as well. I delight in giving to others.

It gets better than that in the gifting and receiving. I recall a scripture saying your gifts will make room for you. Well, it's true. See, my life had been through a lot of readjusting, and that meant departing with the old and welcoming the new. I never thought it was all for destiny's purposes, but now I know it is. I had the opportunity to be thought of in so many ways by others. Someone began dating me. Should I say lightly as I peddle forward?

We crushed on the other. I even thought maybe I was supposed to have him date someone else at my recommendation. This is the part that chokes me up. I used the slogan, Fool, what were you thinking?" It's exactly as I said it. I then came up with another slogan, 'Dating my doctor shoes." Yes, he's also in the medical field as a physician assistant. So that I don't give too much away, I just follow how I set this scene. You already know I'm a scene setter. Follow me, or miss the point. This kind and gentle best friend is not only worth being in my life; I look forward to more of his life in my life. Thinking he would date others, I suggested, was so petty and silly. He's too much of a keeper. See, he also plays the angel list.

You know I can call it "Angels in Vina's Outfield." You know when a person is gentle with a soul of love and compassion. Him. My birthdays were and still are important to me, has always made me very happy with whatever he brought in my direction. I protect that friendship like I protect my family. I can't tell you how thankful I am that one day, he called the office, and then one day, he sat across from me in my office. Now, the rest is just giggles from my view. There's not a key I can't hold that he has not offered me to feel safe with.

I share all this to say something very important. I don't care who you are. I don't care where you have been. I don't care if you are the only one who sees your scars. Beware that God's timing will send the right people to be major key players in the life you live. You will know that they are genuine. You know if they are moochers and manipulators. You know if any love is supposed to be shown or if you are about to be left speechless and in tears. Some folks are only in your life to bring on the bad and evil. Get rid of them quickly. Some people delight in your presence and will go out of their way to make sure they are helping you excel and survive this cruel world. You have a chance to make not only a difference in your life. You have a new chance to make a difference in someone else's life.

If you ever feel the pressure is too much for you at times and need someone to listen to you. Ask God to reveal to you who you need to turn to, and they won't judge you. I know what I'm talking about. Jesus kept me from hurting myself and so many others, and I chose to live today. You can get through that pain you live with. I did it.

I believe you can, and you will survive if you tell your story.

************* **The End*************

QUOTES
By
VINA FLO-Glow

Look at true STRENGTH, not my STRUGGLE.

Don't mistake my color and think I auto—manic (automatically) go hood on you.

MY LIVING IS MY HEALING

GRIND to ALIGN

IT'S OK TO LET GO

YES, IT IS OK!

Why STOP loving you if no one else loves you. Dig deep and love yourself more.

Don't be afraid to Compliment someone. I guarantee they needed it.

Extra special you should feel for acknowledging it.

Being BRAVE before, during, and after the rain is vital.

Why COMPETE with others when your lane is built for you to run. So Run it.

Before you GIVE UP, take about 10 seconds and read up. You will be amazed at what you learn you are capable of doing;

Yes, I am a SURVIVOR! No way can I give up. Face the mirror and reflect that.

Somewhere, SOMEBODY needs your Glow. Here's the secret,

Everyone can have it without limits!

Dream a little…

NOW DREAM BIGGER!

There's no escaping THE TRUTH. How well will you tell it? Be truthful.

If I SINK, I usually look up, and S.O.S., somehow, someone helps me.

RESET is good.

RESET is meaningful.

RESET has a plan.

RESET helps success.

Mind GAMES suck. Be uniquely VOCAL when you spot a trick.

LIFE can be beautiful. It's terrible when ugly people EXIST in it inappropriately.

Let SELF-DISCOVERY be your soul CURRICULUM.

"Woman of SUBSTANCE" isn't harsh. It's the core Truth.

You OWE it to yourself to successfully complete something you started.

*Are you afraid of You? GOD isn't.
He has you in mind.*

See something BIGGER than the situation you are in. You have to see it before you see it.

Raise your STANDARDS; you raise your CONFIDENCE. Raise your VOICE and be heard.

*I don't need A CURE for Love!
Yeah! I am actually enuf.*

When did you stop DREAMING? Never let your dreams disappear from your vision. Give it time and Concentration, and eventually, you see the end goal.

People will be quick to give their opinions about your Life. You decide whether you keep it or trash it. Either way, it's your LIFE, right?

Stop PLAYING Victim. All you do to yourself is victimize where your gifts are inside, needing to be born out of you.

Slow to speak is for you to remember that anger can happen. Think before you open your mouth.

(James 1:19)

There are decent human beings walking the Earth. Are you decent and human?

I can't make this up about me. So watch your THOUGHTS about me because neither can you.

*That Door closed for a Reason.
Watch how wide the other one opens
for you. No peaking.*

Don't be the counterfeit of awakening "Womanhood."

-Toni Jones

Healed from and through with scarcity Thinking.

-*Toni Jones*

Everyone calls me a white girl because I come from the North.

The mirror shows me I'm caramel-complected, have good black hair, wear glasses, and you might find a light-skinned tanned line- just maybe.

Diagnosis: *She's ALIVE*

Extended Diagnosis: *She does SHINE*

I am a business on purpose, NOT a business that makes a busy mess.

Dignified JUST doesn't work for me. If People only knew the Praise I have inside my wackiness. They might catch my wackiness in the end.

My late grandmother often told me, "Anything I DO in this life is already in my hands."

I'm welcome to the next best thing life offers me!"

-Unafraid VNA

Sunshine should bring on a SMILE just as rain often brings on a smile. We need things to grow so that rain is welcome in my Life. I'm growing- SMILING.

Everything is about FAULT. Guess what? I accept it is my fault.

I am before I am anyone else's.

Class is MORE desirable than Trash.

Call forth all the Blessings that belong to YOU!

No more DELAYS by the demon.

Face the truth: not every person you want with u can go with you.

I said he had been loving me. I said she has been -loving him. Watch the Couples goals.

Watch Out; I'm entering a new level of WorthEthic.

Free

If you believe in someone, start by believing in you. That's FREE of charge.

"Power" is better when you understand why you were gifted it!

Look around you as you read with excitement. Didn't you just realize GOD made it away for you?

Let them LAUGH who stand with a silly grin. Let them SMIRK because you walked by. They cannot take your breath away. They are MAD because you took them away.

Keep walking, head up and high.

Always CELEBRATE with you. Thank me later. Let's throw a big party. I invite myself to enjoy the fun.

Make A Toast, Too.

Always REMEMBER it's best to thank people before, during, and in the end. And most importantly, reach out to God with a big thank you.

I can even get mad when folks leave my home, and they shopped my closet for free. SMH

We sabotage and complicate and look completely overrated. Sis, I promise it ain't that deep.

*Getting Smart with Smart People.
(Read that again.)*

There is a reason the Scripture says, Fret Not Thyself. What are we worried about?

The End.